The
Christmas
Visitors

A Norwegian Folktale
Retold and Illustrated by

Jeanette Winter

Pantheon Books

THE CHRISTMAS VISITORS is based on a story collected in eastern Norway by Peter Christen Asbjörnsen, the renowned Norwegian folklorist. Though the traditional version of the tale first appeared in 1852 in *Norske Folkeeventyr* (a pioneer collection of Norwegian folktales compiled by Peter Christen Asbjörnsen and Jörgen Moe), the theme of the bear trainer whose bear drives away the ogre has been traced as far back as the thirteenth century.

All rights reserved under International and Pan-American Copyright Conventions. Published in New York by Pantheon Books, a division of Random House, Inc., and simultaneously in Toronto, Canada, by Random House of Canada Limited. Library of Congress Catalog Card Number: 68-24560

Manufactured in the United States of America

Way up in Finnmark there is a mountain called Dovrefell. In the old days trolls lived in it. Every Christmas Eve the trolls swarmed down in great numbers to celebrate at the house of a poor woodsman called Halvor. And each year, Halvor and his family struggled hard to get everything ready, for they knew the trolls had magic powers and would not hesitate to use them if things were not prepared to their liking. So, first Halvor and his wife cleaned the house up, then they prepared mountains of food for the trolls to feast on.

One year, north of Dovrefell, a lonely trapper caught a big white furry bear. It was such a beautiful beast that he thought he should take it as a Christmas present to the King of Denmark. Early on the day of Christmas Eve he set out on his journey. Hours later, as he passed Halvor's cottage, a heavy snow began to fall and he decided to stop and ask for shelter.

He knocked, and as Halvor slowly opened the door, a delicious smell of roasting meats wafted out onto the cold breeze. Inside, the tables were decked with steaming bowls of creamed porridge, mounds of sausage, shimmering fish, cakes and goodies.

"Oh, Lord bless us!" said Halvor, in answer to the trapper's request for shelter. "We can't put anyone up *now*, for each Christmas Eve the trolls come down in such numbers that they eat every morsel of food in the house and take over our beds to boot! There won't even be room for us."

"Oh well, that won't bother me," said the stranger. "My bear can squeeze under the stove, and I can lie in the closet."

"If that's all you need, you are welcome," said Halvor. "As for me, I'd rather move out to the shed at the edge of the wood." Which was just what he did.

Evening came, and as the tempting smell of the feast drifted from the chimney over Dovrefell, the trolls crept out of the mountain. Flitting from peak to peak, they summoned one another to the feast.

Soon the mountain echoed with their shrieks and trills, and a long procession of trolls began to descend on the valley. First came Old Trond, an ancient troll with a long beard, then the whole crowd of eager trolls swarming behind him. Some were large and some were small, some had long tails and some had none. All were waving silver goblets, ready for the feast.

As they entered the house they broke into a wild dance at the sight of the food. Wine was passed around and poured into each goblet. In their high whining voices, the trolls toasted poor Halvor:

> A feast, a feast, a feast is nice
> With Halvor shivering on the ice.
> And he will have a curse to fear
> If he won't welcome us each year.

Then, head over heels, they fell upon the mounds of food.

They were wallowing in the porridge and swallowing long strings of sausage one after the other, when one of the baby trolls caught sight of the bear's nose sticking out from under the stove.

"Pussy cat! Pussy cat!" he called. "Here's something to eat."

He speared a sausage, toddled over to the stove, and thrust the sizzling morsel into the bear's face. That sausage was hot!

The white bear howled in pain, reared up from under the stove, and muzzled the baby troll right through the window. Growling ferociously, he headed for the table.

At the sight of this the trolls panicked, and shrieking wildly, bolted from their seats and fled like lightning.

Tumbling and stumbling over each other, they raced up the side of Dovre-fell. When they were halfway up the mountain they stopped. Screaming angrily, they hurled a huge boulder at Halvor's cottage. It landed on the edge of the field, where it lies to this day. Then Old Trond opened a door half-hidden among the rocks and they all scrambled into the mountain.

Inside the shed Halvor and his family huddled together. When the crisp night was silent once more, Halvor slowly went to the door to take a peek. Not a troll in sight! He beckoned to his family and they followed him home. The place was a shambles!

In the middle of the table, strewn with leftovers, the great bear was dancing, and his master was singing and clapping time with his hands.

"The trolls have gone," cried the trapper triumphantly. And he told Halvor what had happened.

Halvor thanked the stranger and patted the bear. Then, with what was left of the banquet, they all enjoyed a late Christmas supper. After the meal they sang carols and the children climbed on the bear's back. Full of good food and warmed by the fire, they settled down to sleep.

On Christmas morning, mops, brooms, and buckets in hand, they all helped to put the cottage back in order. Then the trapper got ready to leave.

"Thank you again," said Halvor. "All these years we have scrimped and saved to feed the trolls and now for the first time we are able to have our own Christmas. You are always welcome to our cottage. Please come back soon."

"Who knows? Perhaps I will," replied the trapper, leading his bear out of the house.

A full year went by. And as Halvor was cutting wood at the edge of the forest for Christmas Eve, he heard a screeching from the trees:

"Halvor! Halvor!"

It was Old Trond!

"Here I am," said Halvor.

"Where is your big, nasty cat this year?"

"Still under the stove," Halvor replied, remembering how the bear had frightened the trolls away.

"Is that so?" stammered Old Trond. "And such a bad temper she had!"

"Indeed," said Halvor. "And what's more she now has seven kittens, each bigger and fiercer than she is herself."

"Thank you-oo-oo!" cried the old troll in a small voice that quickly faded off into the woods.

From that time on no one has ever seen or heard from the trolls again. Halvor kept all the silver goblets they left behind, and Christmas at Dovrefell has been peaceful ever since.